Creative Hats

First published in Great Britain, 2023 by C H Press, a division of Creative Hats.

First published in hardback in Hertfordshire in 2023 by C H Books, an imprint of Creative Hats.

This paperback edition published in 2023.

Cover design by: FabsArtDesign.co.uk

Edited by: Mina M, Fantastic Writers & Creative Hats

The Rolling Pumpkin

Mina M

To child refugees - who face all manner of monsters.

Contents

Prologue   7

The Manticore   11

The Simurgh   20

The Azmych   28

The Charybdis   44

The Morpheus   56

The Dragon   69

The Unicorn   83

The Pumpkin   87

Preview Extract   92

Acknowledgements   97

Prologue

'Omid means Hope' the big banner at the top of the wall catches the eye as we enter the great hall for the exhibition. Bold, red blocks of letters make up my name and seem to be buoyant floating in deep, stormy waters. Sea creatures and colourful fish float in and around each letter. A pink jellyfish replaces the point on top of the 'I' and a shark threatens to chop the H from Hope. Sitting on top of the letter M with her legs dangling, is a little black-haired girl clutching her dolly to her chest. Rays of sun break through the dark waves.

'What a thoughtful design Nina.' Maman whispers as she gives my art therapist a kiss on the cheek.

'Is that Rexi?' I point to the huge green dinosaur head poking through the hole in the letter O.

'Why? Don't you like him?' Nina says, tilting her head to have a better look towards where I point.

'Rexi is a dinosaur. He doesn't smile.'

'He is meant to be roaring.'

'His eyes are not angry.'

'How can you tell? Dinosaurs' eyes are all the same.'

'They don't smile,' she says, squinting her eyes and moving a bit closer to the banner. After a while she shrugs, 'It doesn't matter anyway, people are here to see your paintings not mine.' Then winking at me she turns and goes towards the podium where Mrs Palmer our head teacher stands, waiting.

I look around at the quickly filling hall and see, to my horror, that Nina is right. They are already walking around and looking at my paintings, pointing and talking. I see an old lady shaking her white head and a mother lifting her little boy to have a better look at the messy patch of dark blue which was supposed to be a sea monster. Suddenly it feels like a bucketful of icy sea water has been emptied over my head. There is movement inside my belly and I urgently need to wee.

'I want to go home. I need to wee.' I turn around eyes darting to spot the exits. Maman and Baba look at each other horrified.

'Let's go to the toilet first.' Maman says pushing me towards the toilet signs.

'I will go with him. You ask them to hold the speeches for a few minutes.' Baba says as he steers me around as fast as he can.

'Ok, ok, you go quick and don't worry darling it is normal to be nervous.' Maman says her eyes on my pants.

'It's alright son. We will get there on time. Don't worry.'

'Children are the primary victims of wars, violence and other man-made disasters, but their cries for help, their voices and their pleas are rarely heard and what is worse is that more often than not effective solutions to overcome their perils are dismissed under the perception that they are resilient. We assume they'll get over it quickly...' Mrs Palmer says as we finally come out of the toilets and walk slowly back to the hall. It has taken Baba more than ten minutes to calm me down.

'What you see here on the walls of this room is not just some amazing artwork, it is also a story, a story that is unfortunately happening a lot and not heard enough. By displaying these images we are hoping to bring about some understanding of what happens to children like Omid and what they are going through as a result.'

Maman holds my hand and pushes me gently down to sit next to her. Her face reddens when the head teacher thanks me and my family for allowing my work go on display. Not forgetting Nina for her wonderful work in helping me and arranging the exhibition. As I look around the room, I see black haired little girls, toy dinosaurs and sea monsters stepping out of my paintings and crowding around me. Their voices are sharp and clear, talking all at once, eager to remind me of the story.

The Manticore

The Manticore is a legendary persian creature with the head of a human and body of a lion. It has a tail containing venomous spines which are similar to the quills on a porcupine.

The baddies are after my Maman. They want to take her to prison. We have been in hiding at Khaleh Sara's flat for almost a week and it is sooooooo boring! Khaleh Sara is Maman's friend and my parents say she is really brave, putting herself in danger and letting us stay in her flat until things calm down and we can go home. I like Khaleh Sara. She is very kind to me, every evening when

11

she comes home from work, she brings me all sorts of yummy treats and in the evening she tells me funny stories about all the countries she has travelled to and people she has met. I especially like the one about a country she had gone to where people didn't think farting is rude and they would just walk around and fart. I laugh and laugh and ask her to tell me that story many times. Baba says she probably has made it up, he doesn't think there is such a country, but I don't care, I like it.

Khaleh Sara says the only reason she lets us stay in her flat is because she loves Baba's cooking, I know she is joking and that is not the only reason because she winked at me when she said that, but Baba's cooking is the best, only Maman Bozorg can cook better than him. He works in this fancy restaurant where only rich people go and eat.

'I can never afford to go to your restaurant and eat your cooking, so it feels great to have you as a private chef at home.' Khaleh Sara said when she came home the first day to Baba's Barberry Polo rice and saffron chicken.

'Ah, you wouldn't want to go to that restaurant. It is full of uptight, nose in the air, filthy rich people.' Maman always says things like that about the restaurant and no matter how much Baba and I insist, she doesn't go there to eat. I have been there a few times with Uncle Roozbeh, who doesn't mind mixing in with filthy rich people. I enjoy eating at Baba's restaurant. Everybody says the food is great and I want to shout out to tell everybody that my

Baba makes all the lovely food.

Sometimes Baba and Maman Bozorg have a competition and both make super delicious food but we always vote for Maman Bozorg (even if we secretly think Baba's food is better), because Maman Bozorg can't stand losing a cooking competition to someone whose breath still smells of milk, which means my Baba is very young. Baba doesn't mind. He only laughs when Maman Bozorg says things like that. He knows she too is very proud of him and always tells everybody how great a chef he is.

If Khaleh Sara was home all the time, maybe I wouldn't feel so bored, but she has to work and Maman keeps telling me to be careful and not break anything in Kahleh Sara's perfectly decorated flat.

'Sara Jaan please take all these lovely vases and ornaments away and lock them up in a safe place before Omid and his dinosaur destroy them for you.'

Even with almost everything safely put away, it takes my parents a lot of effort to keep me and Rexi, my t-rex toy from roaming around and destroying things. It is easier for me because I get to see all of my favourite programs: Misha and Masha, The Little Red Hat and Tom and Jerry without my parents telling me off for watching too much television, but poor Rexi gets sooooo bored. Unless it is a programme about dinosaurs, he doesn't like watching telly.

We can't even play hide and seek (my favourite) because the flat is too little and there aren't many places to hide, plus we can't make too much noise in case the neighbours hear us. Only drawing and painting and table games are allowed. Baba suggests teaching me chess.

'Imagine Omid sitting down on his bottom for half an hour trying to figure out a move.' Maman said with a laugh.

'I can sit on my bum easy-peasy.' I tell her and sit square on it to show her. But boy oh boy, how boring is chess? You have to learn all those moves and everyone is moving in one way and attacking another and it is not at all clear why the queen moves freely in all directions and as far as she likes, while the king can only move one square at a time. Isn't the king supposed to be the most powerful? After a while, my bum starts tingling and all I really want is to get up and run away, but I see Maman watching me. I keep firm on the seat and try to concentrate.

'When can we go home Maman?'

'I don't know Azizam; it is out of my hands.'

'Why don't you tell the baddies that you are sorry and that you won't write anything in your blog again? Then we can go home.'

'If only things were so easy...' Maman laughs stroking my hair.

'Things are that easy.' I insist. 'When I broke Farzad's new shiny pen, Miss Karimi told me to say I was sorry. I said sorry and promised to let him share my shiny pen, Farzad stopped crying and we were friends again.'

'Were you sorry when you said you were sorry?'

'Yes.'

'That is it then, you say sorry when you think you have done something wrong, but I am not sorry for what I have written.' Maman is ever so stubborn. Even Maman Bozorg and Agha Joon say she is.

'What will happen if we just go home?'

'They will take your Maman to prison.'

'Can I come to prison with you Maman? We can have prison adventures; we can find all the escape routes and then have an amazing escape adventure.'

'You and your adventure craze.' Maman hugs me tight and lifts me up. She knows I can no longer stay on my bum.

'I think we may have the biggest ever adventure soon. If things don't get sorted we may have to leave the country.' Baba says, but he doesn't sound very excited.

Maman is right I am crazy about adventures; I like doing exciting things and going to places where there are possibilities of meeting someone or doing something exciting. The 'grownups' have to invent fancy names or make up adventure stories to get me out of the house. Some of the adventures they come up with are fun but most turn out to be no adventures at all. The Great Bazaar Adventure they promised me once, was nothing but another boring shopping trip to a very big old bazaar somewhere in Tehran.

The Adventure Through Underworlds, sounded so spectacular and made me imagine meeting lots of underworld beasts and creatures, (I even asked Baba if we might see Hades the God of the underworld, the one that I had seen in Hercules), was no big deal at all just a long ride on the metro to one of Maman's many secret meetings.

One adventure that I particularly liked was The Protest Adventure which was held in one of the city's big squares and lots of people were holding up banners and shouting things.

I wanted to have a banner too, so someone gave me one with some red writing. I was so happy to have a banner that I held it as high as I could and went round shouting, 'Free the dragons!' I had a book in which people had banners in their hands and demanded to get rid of the dragon and the dragon was good so I came up with 'Free the dragon,' as a thing. People started to notice me and laughed when they heard what I was saying. Baba came running to me and told me to stop talking nonsense and shout something that had anything to do with the protest.

'Like what?'

'Say - we children want to go to school.'

'But school is boring, I don't want to say that.'

'Ok, say we children want to play.'

'Can I say we want more dinosaurs?'

But there was no time to say anymore. Suddenly there were lots of policemen everywhere and they started pushing people around and hitting them with their sticks. People were screaming and running. Baba quickly picked me up, pulled the banner from my hand and threw it to the side of the road and shouted to Maman to come this way. Everybody was running around; they were getting in each other's way and bumping together. Over Baba's shoulder I watched the policemen swing their sticks in the air and bring them down on people's heads and arms very hard, some people had blood on their faces and some were being dragged into the police vans. My parents ran through the crowd and out towards a quiet back street where they stopped a taxi and jumped inside, ordering the driver to go to my grandparents' house which was close by.

When we got there I told Agha Joon about my adventure. I told him it was the best adventure ever, but he was not happy at all, he didn't even laugh about my silly dragon chant.

'How dare you put this child in danger?" He looked at Maman and Baba with angry eyes. I had only ever seen his eyes like once before, when I broke his DVD player by pushing two DVDs in at the same time.

'Those poor kids who work on the streets are always in danger. Shouldn't we care about them?' Maman asked. She was angry too.

'Omid is a child. He should stay out of things that are not suitable for children and protest is certainly not an adventure, not in Iran.'

I didn't want Agha Joon to look at me the way he looked at Maman and Baba, so I went to Maman Bozorg, curled up on her soft, wobbly lap and asked her to tell me the story of Kadoo Qelqelizan, The Rolling Pumpkin:

"Once upon a time there was an old lady who lived all by herself in a small cottage at the bottom of a hill. Her only daughter had married and moved away. The old lady missed her daughter and wanted to go and visit her, but her daughter's house was right at the top of the hill and there were many wild creatures living among the huge trees that covered that hill. It would be quite dangerous to travel this way. One day she was missing her beloved daughter so much that she no longer could wait, so she decided to take the risk

18

and go anyway. As she went up the winding road through the thickly grown forest she came face to face with a big, fierce wolf. The wolf bared his terrible sharp teeth and came slowly towards the old woman "Come here you old lady, I am so hungry, I want to gobble you up."

"Oh, please Mr Wolf don't eat me," said the old lady shaking with fear, "You see I am very skinny, there isn't really much meat on me to make you full. I am on my way to visit my daughter. If you let me go, I will go to my daughter and she will feed me lots of lovely things. I will eat Khoresht Bademjoon (aubergine and chicken stew), I will eat fluffy saffron rice and Khoresht Fesenjoon (pomegranate and walnut stew) and I will become fat and juicy, then coming back you can eat me."

"Ah," the wolf thought. "You are not lying are you?"

"No of course not. I would never lie to you."

"Ok then," said the wolf. "You can go, but don't be too long, I am really hungry."

The old lady quickly got away from the wolf and went further up the ever-winding road…"

The Simurgh

Simurgh is a benevolent, mythical bird from Persian literature and mythology. It is thought to serve as a mediator between the sky and earth.

I don't want to leave my home, my toys, my friends, my Maman Bozorg and Agha Joon and go on an adventure through other countries. My parents say we have no choice, we can't stay in hiding forever and the baddies still want to punish my Maman for writing in her blog.

'I haven't written anything.' I say, 'Nobody wants to put me in prison, I can stay with Maman Bozorg and Agha Joon.'

'Maman Bozorg and Agha Joon are very old, they won't be able to look after you. Plus we can't go without you, this is our family's greatest adventure, it won't be fun if you don't go with us.'

Maman Bozorg and Agha Joon have come to say goodbye to us, Uncle Roozbeh is here too. He will drive us somewhere and there we can meet the guy who is going to help us. Maman Bozorg has cooked my favourite Halva for me to take on the journey.

'Now, keep some for your journey Azizam, don't finish it all, you'll get stomach ache.'

'I love your Halva Maman Bozorg.'

Agha Joon gave me his old Walkman and a tape of my favourite songs so I can listen to music during my journey. This is exciting because Agha Joon would not usually let me play with his Walkman. He always said I would destroy it in no time. Maman and Uncle Roozbeh always make fun of Agha Joon for being old fashioned and not letting go of his old Walkman. But Agha Joon says the new gadgets are very complicated and not as good.

'Twenty thousand dollars is a lot of money, how on earth can we find that much money so soon?'

'Don't worry Brother, I will knock on a few doors and try to get a loan.'

'You can sell both our cars, Maryam's jewellery and the furniture and whatever there is to be sold really.'

'The carpets will fetch a good price, they are handmade. They were our wedding gift from your parents.'

'Don't sell my dinosaurs Uncle Roozbeh. You can sell my Lego, police cars, trains and fire engines because I don't play with them anymore but put all my dinosaurs and monster tracks in a box and take them to Maman Bozorg to keep them for when I come back.'

'As you command my Omid.' Uncle Roozbeh says smiling. He always talks that way to me when he wants to joke. Uncle Roozbeh is the coolest uncle in the whole wide world. He knows magic tricks, plays guitar and rides on a super cool motorbike. He lets me go with him on his motorbike to music rehearsals, but I have to promise not to tell Maman and Baba, because they get mad if they know I have been riding on a motorbike. Especially on Tehran's dangerous roads. When I grow up I want to have long hair like him and put my sunglasses on top of my head just the way he does.

'Don't you worry Azizam; I will keep your toys safe for you.' Maman Bozorg gives me a nice squeeze. I am sitting on her lap, cuddling up to her warm and soft breast.

She keeps kissing me and smelling me and squeezing me, I think she has missed me a lot. I ask her to tell me the Kadoo qelqelizan story. She is the best storyteller, even better than Maman.

"... Halfway up, she came face to face with a large, furry, stripy tiger, who is inching slowly towards her, his big orange eyes fix on her unblinking,

"Come here old woman." he growled, "I am starving, I must eat you up at once."

"But please dear tiger, don't eat me, as you can see I am but skin and bones, there is hardly any meat on me to satisfy your hunger. Let me go visit my daughter. She will feed me Khoresht Bademjoon and Morgh o Fesenjoon and fluffy saffron rice. I will eat all sorts of yummy things and soon fatten up. Then on the way back you can eat me."

"Ah." the tiger pondered. "You are not lying are you?"

"No of course not. I would never lie to you."

"Ok then." said the tiger. "You may go but come back soon because I am very hungry. I can't wait too long.."

'Maman Bozorg, when I go to Englestan, will you come

and visit me?'

'You bet I will, but what if the big bad wolf or the striped tiger or his majesty the lion see me? I can't possibly say I am too skinny can I?'

'No you can't. You have enough meat on you to satisfy all the wild creatures in the forest.' Agha Joon says with a laugh.

'You mean old man.' Maman Bozorg growls and pretends to be hurt.

We met the agent who is supposed to help us get out of the country in a cafe near Uromia. He is short, fat, bald and reminds me of Matilda's father in the film I have seen with my friend Sina. While the grown-ups talk about our journey and money and other boring things, I eat my bread and cheese and play with Rexi. I know he is hungry and offer him some bread and butter but he tells me not to be silly because he is a T-Rex and T-Rexes only eat meat.

'All I care about is the safety of my sister and her family. I will assure you that I will get the money sorted very soon and will put it in the deposit account until they reach their destination – safely.'

'Don't worry. We will look after them, we have to. One of us is always traveling with them and if they are in any danger, we will be too. But please be discreet about my details. You know we are valuable people and almost every government is trying to find us.' He laughs at his own joke even when nobody sees a joke in what he says.

Soon we have to say goodbye to Uncle Roozbeh and go with Matilda's father.

'Be strong my dear Omid, look after your parents for me.' He gives me a final squeeze and puts me down. His face is wet. I tell him to say goodbye to Rexi too, which he does and then gets into his car and drives away.

'Come on young man; get into the car we have to go.' Matilda's father gives me a gentle push and we climb into his car. He talks and laughs, laughs and talks, while Baba who is sitting in the front seat, listens and listens and listens and sometimes pretends to laugh with him. Maman reads books to me and tells me more about Englestan and the big museum in London where there are huge dinosaurs that can roar.

After driving for hours, Matilda's father takes us to a house where there is another family like us, waiting to go on their own adventure. They have a little girl who is a bit younger than me. She is hugging her dolly tight to her chest.

'Look how lucky you are young man. This beautiful young lady is going to travel with you all the way to

Engelestan. I bet by the time you get there you two will be in love.' Matilda's father laughs heartily at his own joke again.

I don't feel lucky to have a little girl and her boring dolly travel with us, a boy with dinosaurs or monster trucks would be a lot more fun. The little girl takes a look at me and Rexi and goes and hides behind her mother's legs. The grownups say a few more things about us eyeing each other and things that I don't understand and then go back to talking about their more serious things.

'Now have some lunch and get yourselves some sleep because tonight you won't get a chance to sleep at all.' Matilda's father tells them before he leaves. He could still be heard talking and chuckling as he goes down the stairs and into his car.

After lunch, the grownups want to sleep. Sheerin, the little girl, pretends that she is putting her dolly to sleep. Rexi and I are bored and we don't feel sleepy at all, so we start prowling around looking for something fun to do. We go closer to Sheerin and her dolly. Rexi tries to scare them with a mighty roar. Sheerin screams, picks up her dolly and squeezes her in her arms. I am told off for making so much noise and not letting anyone sleep. I sit in a corner and try to read my book as Baba suggests. First I read quietly and in a whisper so that only Rexi can hear, but soon I forget to be quiet and my reading gets louder with lots of gestures and voice changes. I am trying to mimic the way my

Maman reads to me. I realise that Sheerin is looking at me and very soon she comes close enough to see the pictures in the book and starts asking questions.

The Azmych

Azmych is a Turkish mythical evil road spirit that causes disorientation and leads people aimlessly around.

'Now, we have to be very, very quiet. No shouting, no calling each other, no talking and no crying.' Here the guide that Matilda's father said was a very good guide and would take us safely to the other side of the border stops talking and looks at me and Sheerin for a moment to make sure we understand and then continues.

'There are all sorts of guards and armed people around the frontier and if we make any noise they will hear us and we will be in terrible trouble. Sometimes they don't even care who is passing by, they just open fire and shoot. It is for everybody's safety that we must all stay very quiet. If anyone needs to say something to either me or my colleague, pass the message to the person in front of you or behind you. Don't come out of your line because we may lose you. Make sure that you keep your eyes on the person who is walking ahead of you. Is that clear? Any questions?'

He looks rough with his long beard and uncombed hair. In his big bony hand he is holding a long, knotty stick which is supposed to help him walk but the way he turns it around and points it here and there makes me feel scared. I think Sheerin feels the same because I see her hiding her face behind her father's back.

Baba squeezes my shoulders gently to show that all is ok and whispers into my ear, 'This is a real adventure, ha?'

I nod.

At first we all start walking quietly. I am holding Baba's hand and trying to watch my steps as it is too dark to see anything, but soon I start to get real tired and find it harder and harder to climb the steep hill. Sheerin is already riding on her father's back, clutching her dolly tightly to her chest. I wish my Baba would carry me on his back, but I don't want to ask because I have promised uncle Roozbeh that I would be a big boy and look after Maman and Baba. Poor Baba is already carrying a big backpack on his back.

'This is a stupid adventure.' I say after a while. I feel like crying. Baba says it is ok. He notices I am tired. He says he can carry me on his back. After swapping his rucksack with Maman, he lets me climb on top of the smaller rucksack he is going to carry from then on. I sit on top of the rucksack and am told to hold on tight to the strings. Baba's warm back, and his rhythmic breathing soon lulls me to sleep.

It is getting light when we finally stop walking. The guide takes us to a barn and tells us to make ourselves a bed on the hay and get some sleep. It feels cold and uncomfortable, but nobody even grumbles. We curl up close to each other and fall asleep. Some hours later I wake up and start looking around to see what is going on in the barn. Piles and piles of hay is stacked everywhere and chicken are pecking their way through the fallen hay looking for food. I spot a big grey cat sitting high up on a beam looking down with suspicious eyes at us, maybe thinking, 'what are these strange people doing in my house?'

I take Rexi by his tiny arm and we go exploring the barn.

'What a lovely adventure Rexi.' I say excitedly jumping from stacks of hay and chasing chickens around the barn. Sheerin and her dolly soon join us and we make such a fuss that the grownups wake up grumbling and tell us to please be quiet because unlike us they haven't had a wink of sleep all night and they are dead tired.

'Look, look Baba, Maman, look we found eggs. There are eggs here. The chickens have laid eggs. Can we have them for breakfast please?'

'I don't know.' Says a very sleepy Baba rubbing his eyes and looking around 'We have to wait for the guides to come back and tell us what to do.'

'But it is late and we are hungry. When will they come back? What if they never come back. We will starve to death.'

Sure enough the guy and his friends come back very soon, bringing us breakfast and hot, sweet tea. There are no cooked eggs but I don't mind and gulp the hot bread and homemade jam down happily, washing it all down with sweet tea.

***

Unfortunately our farm adventure soon comes to an end and another long, boring car journey starts. We are told we are going to go to Istanbul where the preparations for our journey will start.

'Preparations?' Sheerin's mum quietly whispers into Maman's ear. 'I thought we were already halfway through this bloody journey.'

Sheerin's mum grumbled all night as we walked. She said the walk was barbaric and it was killing her back and her legs. She cried when she broke one of her long, brightly coloured nails trying to stop herself falling down as she trips over a big root trailing out of the ground.

'This is not a good sign. A broken nail is bad luck. That is the last thing we need right now.' She said wiping her tears away with the back of her other hand.

'Don't worry darling. Don't pay much attention to this nonsense. Keep walking before the Qachaghchi (agent) finds out we have stopped?' Sheerin's dad kissed his wife's fingers and gave her a small push to make her move.

She is still in a bad mood and keeps talking about her broken nail and how the rough journey has messed up her hairdo. I can see from Maman's face that she doesn't have any patience for these kinds of things. Maman keeps her nails short and only paints them when she is going to a party or there is a special occasion. Neither does she make any fuss over her hair.

In the car I ask Maman to tell Sheerin and I the story of the Rolling pumpkin again:

"......*The old lady went up the hill as fast as her old legs allowed her to go. She already could see the top of the hill and hoped that she would soon get there without any more dangerous encounters. But as she was happily dreaming of meeting her daughter and eating a hearty meal, she heard a terrible roar. The lion was larger and hungrier than the other two. He was standing on a rock, all ready to jump and gobble the poor old lady up. "Come here old woman, I want to eat you up, I am very hungry."*

"But your majesty what would be the use of eating a skinny old thing like me, I can hardly be enough to fill you up, why don't you let me go and visit my daughter. She will feed me all sorts of lovely things, I will eat Khoresht Bademjoon, I will eat Morgh o Fesenjoon, I will eat fluffy saffron rice and then I will be nice and chubby and on the way back you can eat me."

"Are you lying to me?"

"Of course not, how dare I lie to a great king like yourself."

"Ok then you may go, but come back soon, I am waiting for you..."

***

Istanbul is full of light and sound. The traffic there is as bad as Tehran's. On the pavements people of all sorts mingle and walk around. Most women don't wear head scarves here, some of them are holding hands with a man. I look at Maman and realise that she and Sheerin's mum have taken their scarves off.

'Aren't they scared that the police could arrest them for not wearing head scarves?'

'No. In Turkey, women are allowed to walk around with a bare head.'

We stop somewhere by the sea to have dinner. The sea is blue and shiny and the sand yellow and soft. Sheerin and I gobble down our dinner quickly so we can run to play on the beach. We bury Rexi and pretend to dig up dinosaur fossils. Dolly doesn't want to get her pretty dress messed up, so she just sits there looking at us with her blue, wide eyes. Then we make some sandcastles which aren't that good because we don't have any buckets and spades.

As the sun begins to set it turns the sea sparkly gold. even the sky looks aflame. The waves come into the shore with a splash and bring a lot of sand and empty shells with them. Big and small boats cross the sea making loud honking noises. As if not wanting to be left out, the white birds circle over them adding their own shrieking sounds to all other noises. Maman and Baba stand at the edge of the water watching the sun turn orange as it almost falls into the other side of the sea. Maman's hair is being blown by the wind and looks like a flag. Baba carefully gathers all the blown away hair in his hands and combs through it with his fingers before letting it fall down Maman's back again. It doesn't take long before the playful wind picks it all up again and throws it around. Sheerin stands up and shakes her head.

'I want my hair to look like a flag too.'

'Yours is not as long as Maman's.'

'My hair is very long. Look.' She tilts her head back and shows me how long her hair would fall on her back.

'When I grow old like your Maman, my hair will be here.' She touches behind her knees.

'Then you can have a big flag in the wind.'

I like Sheerin's hair. It is black and shiny and very soft. Sheerin's mum doesn't want her hair to be blown in the wind. She puts her hands on top of her head to stop the wind messing it around. She likes to keep her hair tidy and in good shape.

I would love to stay by the sea and watch the sun go into the water. But our guide says we have to go because we want to be in the house before dark.

The house he is talking about is an old, ugly place in a basement with only two small windows and very few bits of furniture. From the windows we can only see people's feet walking on the street. It gets very busy in the mornings and evenings. We are strictly forbidden to open those tiny windows during daytime even if the smell in the house is very bad. Neighbours don't know there are so many of us living here and we shouldn't make too much noise, otherwise they might report us to the police. A family with two young children are already there. They said they had been here for a week waiting for their journey to be sorted. We join them waiting.

'What will happen if the police find us here?'

'They will send us back to Iran. Then we will be in trouble.'

'I won't be in trouble. I will go straight to Agha Joon and Maman Bozorg.'

For hours on end we watch legs and feet passing by the little window that shines a bit of light in what is supposed to be the living room. We try to come up with people's stories, by watching their feet. There are beautiful, fancy shoes clip clopping on the pavement, alongside worn out, dirty boots with holes in them. Occasionally somebody stops there for a few seconds, probably reading a text or checking directions on a map. The only person who stands there for more than a few seconds is a young girl (the grown-ups say they guess she is young because she has beautiful soft legs and wears a pair of red converses which are apparently fashionable among young people. She stands there for what seems like ten minutes, shifting from one leg to another and turning this way and that. A discussion brakes out among the grown-ups to guess who she was waiting for.

'For her boyfriend obviously.'

'What a strange place for a rendezvous.'

'Or maybe she is simply waiting for her friend or Mother.'

'Maybe she is just tired and standing there to rest.'

'I am sure there are dozens of better places to rest in Istanbul.'

Finally a pair of jeans bottomed with white trainers approaches her, getting close enough for the knees to touch briefly. We hear excited, raised noises coming through the tiny window, suggesting the two might be arguing and after a few seconds the two pairs of legs disappear putting an end to the brief excitement they had brought to our eventless, boring life.

In the mornings and afternoons children our age wearing grey or black trousers or skirts and smart black shoes go by our window, obviously on their way to school or on their way home from school. How I miss my school and my friends. I can imagine Sina and Parviz in their school uniforms traveling to school together and talking about football. I wonder if they remembered me at all.

The guides come in everyday, bringing us food and telling us we have to wait longer. Grown-ups argue with them, getting angry and telling them off for not doing their job properly and the guides just shrug and tell them their bosses are responsible. Grown-ups become more and more irritable and shout at us for no reason.

'Stop making that noise.'

'Tell your son to stop roaring.'

'Stop slamming that door.

'Turn down your music.'

'Stop fighting over that truck.'

'Why don't you teach your daughter to talk instead of scream?'

'Why don't YOU tell your son to stop harassing my little girl?'

Between shouting at us and at each other, the grown-ups do what they like best, talk. They talk about their plans for when they reach Kharej, they talk about their jobs, their families, films, music, football and lots of other stuff. I only half listen to them as I sit on Maman's lap trying to go to sleep. My ears usually prick up when I hear an interesting word or something that sounds nice.

'In 1988 the government arrested so many political dissidents that the prisons were overflowing. We had to share a small cell between twenty of us. The only way we could cope was by following a very strict routine that we had agreed between us. That way, we not only managed to stay sane but we actually benefited from each other's knowledge. Jokingly we called it the *University of Prison.*

Mr Hashemi who was a lot older than the other parents enjoys talking about his past and how he survived six years of prison.

'That's it.' Maman says loudly, interrupting Mr Hashemi and jolting me out of my sleepy trance. 'That is what we should do here. We should schedule our days to keep ourselves busy and to learn from each other.' She sounds very excited.

'But we are not going to be here for too long I hope.'

'I hope not. But we don't know how long we will be and instead of going mad and screaming at each other we can actually make use of our time.'

Maman makes a timetable and writes down what

39

we should do every morning, afternoon and evening. Almost every hour of the day is allocated to some activity or another. It starts with physical exercise at eight o'clock in the morning.

'Now take your places please and allow some space for arm and leg movements.' Sheerin's mum says as she plugs in her mobile phone and finds the right music.

'My mammy is a personal trainer at the gym. She is very good.' Sheerin proudly explains to us children as we take our places in the first row.

The music goes boom boom boom ba ba ba boom and Sheerin's mum makes us do a slow march on the spot and then all sorts of other moves. Some of the moves are like the ones we do at school. It is funny to see our parents huffing and puffing as they kick their legs and punch the air.

After breakfast the lessons begin. Mr Hashemi teaches us maths and science in the morning. He makes people take off their socks to help us add and subtract. We make a lot of steam in the kitchen when he tries to show us how rain is made.

Nastaran Khanom, Mehrdad and Mahsa's mum use the quiet hour after lunch (when the grown-ups like to nap) to teach us drawing and sketching. In the afternoons Maman uses her dictionary to teach us English.

'Sheerin can be your little helper. She has been going to English classes for a long time.' Sheerin's mum says stroking her daughter's long hair. 'She speaks very good English. Don't you my darling?'

Our favourite class is cooking class in the late afternoon. Baba has asked the guide to bring us food materials instead of ready meals and we have lots of fun cooking, especially when we make cookies and cakes. Yum.

Even us children have to teach something. I talk about dinosaurs. I tell them how dinosaurs lived for millions of years and how huge they were, how some of them have to swallow stones to help them digest their food. I also tell them how a huge meteor hit the earth and wiped the dinosaurs out. Everybody said my class was very good and they had learned a lot about dinosaurs.

Between classes we play musical statues or have running competitions or whatever other physical activities Maman can think of.

'We need to do as many physical activities as possible. The kids' energy must be spent or we're doomed.'

Even after all that we are still fully awake and need more entertainment. With no television or internet in the house our parents need to think hard to find some old-fashioned games to fill our evenings. Mr Hashemi having grown up with no TV has many ideas. My favourite is called, *The King and the Minister.* A match box is all we need. Someone would throw the box and depending on what side the box lands the thrower becomes king, minster or thief.

'My king, I have caught this man stealing, how do you suggest I should punish him?' The minister announces when all three parties have been known.

'Ah, stealing is no good. He must be punished. I suggest you make him jump and croak like a frog. That teaches him not to steal anymore.' The king smirks looking at the miserable thief who is waiting for his punishment.

We all take to the floor laughing as Baba (who is the unfortunate thief) croaks and jumps around the room.

'What? A woman stealing jewellery? Punish her by making her dance for us.'

We clap and sing as Nastaran Khanom, does a belly dance for us.

I want to become a king and make everybody roar like a dinosaur but I never get the chance.

Maman is our favourite storyteller. She knows many stories and makes-up noises for every character and sometimes plays out the actions. She makes everything sound funny.

" ... Finally the old lady managed to get away from all those wild animals and reached her daughter's house. There her daughter cooked her Khoresht Bademjoon, She made her Fesenjoon and chicken with fluffy saffron rice and loads of other yummy food. She Enjoyed the clean, fresh air and the company of her daughter and her son in law. As time went by she started to put on weight and plump up. No longer only skin and bones, she was in no particular hurry to go back home, not with all those wild, hungry animals waiting to gobble her up.

"What can I do?" she asked her daughter "I can't stay here forever, I must go back, but I am scared to come face to face with the lion or tiger or wolf again."

Her daughter thought for a while then she came up with a great idea. She went to the farm and bought a giant pumpkin and carefully cut the top. She carved the insides out and made enough room for her mother to squeeze in. Then she helped her mother get in, secured the top and took her to the top of the hill to roll her down ... "

The Charybdis

In Greek mythology, the Charybdis is a sea monster who takes the form of a large whirlpool. It is capable of dragging whole ships under water.

We are going on a boat trip! Yay!! We are going to the sea to get on a boat and cross the sea to the other side. Sheerin, Mahsa, Mehrdad and I are very excited, we keep chanting, 'We are going on a boat ride'.

Our parents are very quiet. I guess after talking nonstop for the past three days, they have used up every word and have nothing else to say. They just sit there in the dark van staring at nothing. Even Sheerin's mammy is not moaning about her frizzy hair and her peeling nail colour.

I think our parents wanted to fly in an airplane. They have been arguing with the smuggler all week.

'But we had a deal, we paid you to take us by air.' I heard Baba tell the man one day.

'I know, and we have done all we could to make that happen. But the custom in Turkish airports are taking extra measures these days to stop us. We have had quite a few of our clients caught. Even one of our agents was almost caught. We don't want to take any more risks.'

'The sea journey is very dangerous. You must have heard the news.'

'We have been taking people across safely for months and nothing has happened to any of our groups. The whole boat ride is not more than a few miles.'

I don't understand why Baba is so scared of going on a boat. He was born and grew up in the port city of Bushehr in the south of Iran. His father worked as a fisherman and Baba had helped his father all the time. He loves sea adventures. He told me himself. He even said one day when I am older we can go on a sea adventure together. Maybe we could take uncle Sohrab too.

'Don't worry Baba' I try to make him happy again 'Boat rides are almost as fun as airplanes. Remember how much fun we had in Uncle Sohrab's boat? And anyway, the Qachaqchi says we can still go on the airplane somewhere else.'

'Ok my son.' Baba tries to smile and ruffles my hair, but I can see he still wants to go on an airplane.

When Grandfather died, Uncle Sohrab took over the fishing business. He used to say unlike some (he meant my Baba), he was proud of being a fisherman. Even when he married, his wife moved in and they all lived in their house with Old Mama. Him and Baba told me funny stories about their childhoods and how they played with their friends in the sea and how they tried to find pearls and become rich. Baba and Uncle Sohrab once showed me a big cliff and told me that they had jumped from up there into the sea. I wanted to do that but they said I was too young and when I am older they would let me try. When Uncle Sohrab saw me swim in the sea for the first time he said I was a natural swimmer.

'This boy has our blood running in his veins.' he said proudly.

Poor Baba was very sad when we left Iran without saying goodbye to Uncle Sohrab and Old Mama. They live so far away from Tehran; they couldn't come to visit us in hiding. When we got to Istanbul, Baba called them on the phone and cried. He said he missed them. Maman and I tried to be very nice to him and make him feel better.

'Baba, does the boat we are going on make a honking sound like Uncle Sohrab's?'

'I don't know son.'

'Do you think it has a little lamp to light the way?'

'Maybe'

'Boat rides are good adventures aren't they?'

'I suppose they are.'

Maman suggests that she tells us a story, to keep us quiet for a few minutes.

"… The giant pumpkin rolled down the hill and went rolling through the winding, steep way, speeding up as it rolled and bumping into a rock or a tree trunk from time to time. The old lady prayed to all gods that she would not encounter the wild creatures of the forest along her way. But no matter how passionately she prayed, sure enough very soon her fear realised and the rolling pumpkin was stopped by a mighty paw.

"Tell me roly-poly pumpkin, have you seen an old lady?" roared the lion as he said this.

"No." said the old lady inside the pumpkin "No, I swear to the gods of the fairies and all the feathered birds that I have not seen an old lady. Now could you please give me a push so I can carry on rolling down the hill."

The Lion was not convinced. He kept his powerful paw on the pumpkin a bit longer and examined the pumpkin all around. But he could not find anything and could see no use in keeping a useless pumpkin any longer. So he gave it a mighty push and the pumpkin rolled even faster down the winding road ..."

When we finally get there, nothing is as I imagined. There is no pier, no boats parked anywhere and no lights at all. It is all darkness and even though I can smell the salty air of the sea and hear the waves crashing onto the shore, I cannot see anything. The agent tells us to wait behind a mound of sand and be absolutely quiet while the men prepare the dinghy.

'What's a dinghy? 'I ask Maman in a whisper.

'A small, inflatable boat' Maman whispers back.

'Why do we have to travel in a dinghy?'

'I don't know my son.'

Baba and Sheerin's father and Mr Hashemi have

gone with the agent to help him get the dinghy ready.

Maman puts her arms around me and cuddles me close to keep me warm. Other Mums cuddle their children too. We sit there waiting in silence. I hide my face in Maman's bosom to get away from the cold wind that blows sand into my eyes. Maman smells good and her arms are so warm and comfy around me that I start to feel drowsy and almost fall asleep when finally Sheerin's father comes to fetch us. We are not alone. There is already a crowd gathered by the dinghy when we get there and I hear Baba arguing with the agent.

'But this dinghy is not strong enough to carry all of us.' I can't see Baba in the dark but I feel his anger from the way he raises his voice and the way his words shoot in his throat. Baba knows all about boats and seas, but the agents want to do things their own way and won't listen to my Baba.

'Listen all. We don't have time to argue. We are getting into this boat and sailing away, if you want to go with us, you can join us, if not you can stay and find your own way across or back.'

There is a murmur of talking and growling among grown-ups. They are scared to get on the dinghy, yet they don't dare to stay behind in the middle of nowhere on a cold and foreign beach. The agent who told us not to make the slightest noise suddenly shouts at people around them and urges everyone to get in quickly or else stay away and let others get in.

There is a lot of movement and rustling as people put on their life jackets and help their children with theirs. Baba helps me to put on my life jacket and reminds me how the whistle works.

'Remember what Uncle Sohrab told you? You are a natural swimmer. He was proud of you and so am I. If you did end up in the sea, stay calm and swim towards the lights. Don't panic, don't look for others, and just keep swimming.' Baba gives me a hug and lifts me into the dinghy.

I am confused, excited and scared all at the same time. I don't understand why everybody has to listen to two crazy men who keep shouting and shoving others around.

Maman and Baba sit very close on either side of me and hold my hands. From the way they squeeze my fingers a bit harder than normal, I know they are nervous. As people get in, the dinghy gets heavier and heavier, sinking deeper into the water. From the sound of lapping water across the sides of the dinghy, it is clear that half of the sides have already gone under.

With a moan and shake, the dinghy jerks forward, proceeding into the heart of the dark, cold sea which has nothing in common with Istanbul's turquoise waters we played by only a couple of weeks ago. The waves are strong and high and as we go further away from the shore, they become stronger and bigger.

All around us stormy monsters gang up with the wind to roar and splash at us, playing with our little dinghy, breathing their horrible cold breath on us and laughing their malicious laugh.

'It is going to sink.' People start to scream in panic.

'Drop all your bags. Quick. Before we sink.' Shouts the Qachaqchi desperately trying to reduce the weight of the dinghy.

No one wants to drop their bags, instead they cling to them and ignore what the man says. Suddenly he gets up and reaches for the bags within reach and starts throwing them overboard. Us being closest to him our bag is the first he picks up and throws into the sea with a big thud.

'Noooooooooooooooooo.' I scream with all my might 'Rexi is in that bag. Get him out.'

Before getting in the dinghy, Baba persuaded me to put Rexi in the bag. He told me it was better to have both my hands free in case I need to swim. I agreed to put Rexi into the bag, but only till we got to the other side. Rexi didn't want to leave me but I told him that he would be safe and warm there.

As our bag is swallowed by a roaring wave, I scream louder and try to wriggle free from my parent's grip to jump overboard and rescue my dinosaur.

Realising that my parents are not able to keep me quiet, the Qachaqchi grabs hold of my arm firmly and tells me in a horrible scary voice that if I don't shut up this same second, he will throw me into the sea too.

I am frightened by this man's loud voice in my ear and his painful grip on my arm. I bury my face in Maman's arms and cry. Maman and Baba both hold me tight, patting my back and kissing me. They too are crying.

I cry bitterly into Maman's neck, saying over and over how I hate this horrible adventure. Maman repeatedly apologizes for making us all go through this horrible journey and tries to reassure me that everything will be alright. But everything is not going to be alright. Everything is going badly wrong, The sea is getting angrier and angrier, the waves become higher and louder and the dinghy gets so full of water that it could sink any minute. Baba and other men have to jump into the sea and hold on to the sides of the dinghy in order to keep it floating. The rest of the passengers try to empty the dinghy of the water that is rising inside it. Some people pray and others cry.

A powerful wave lifts our boat high up in the air, I look at the direction where Sheerin and her mum are sitting. Her huge eyes widen as big as a bush baby. Other than her frightened oversize eyes I can't see much else in the dark but sense her fear and can imagine she is clutching her dolly to her chest. I long for Rexi.

Everything goes dark.

We lose touch with Baba and other men hanging by the dinghy. We are sent into the sky and down crashing into the mouth of the sea. People scream and call each other. I try to hold on to Maman's hand but our fingers unclench as if by a strong, purposeful hand.

'Omiiiiiiiiiiiiiiiiid.' My name echoes back from the waves that claim her.

After a couple of slow-motion summersaults I hit the water. It is piercing cold. The sharp salty water makes its way through my open mouth and nose, stings my throat.

Coming out of the first wave, gasping for breath and coughing out the water, I try to look for Maman and Baba, but each time I open my eyes the playful waves hit me in the face and force me to shut them again. I feel with my feet and my hands for something, anything to cling on to, but each time I end up splashing the bottomless water. I feel like a floating rubber toy being taken for play by a giant monster.

Remembering what Baba had told me, I try to gather all my strength and overcome the waves. I breathe in, stretch my arms, position my body atop of the water and start to swim, keep my eyes on a spot where I imagine I can see some lights twinkling far far away.

As I kick the water back, I see Uncle Sohrab's proud smile, *"It is in your blood young nephew. You are a natural swimmer."*

I don't know how long I swim and where in that vast sea I am. I still imagine I hear voices and see lights. I find my whistle and blow as hard as I can. I remember how much fun Sheerin, Mahsa, Mehrdad and I had trying out our whistles back in the basement in Istanbul.

The Qachaqchi had brought the life jackets for everyone and asked us to try them on and get used to them. Baba took on the job of teaching us how to wear them and how to use the whistle. We kids drove all the grown-ups crazy by going around the little flat whistling and playing lifeguards and policemen, Worried that the neighbours would hear us somebody took the life jackets away from us and put them somewhere we couldn't reach them.

I thought about Sheerin and the others and wondered what might have happened to them. I wished we had never left that basement. We may have felt like prisoners there but at least we were not drowning.

Exhaustion is taking over me. I fight hard to keep my eyes open and concentrate. My arms and legs ache, a tightening sensation grabs hold of my chest making it harder and harder to breath. Something inside me wants to give up trying, close my eyes and let the waves take me wherever they want. Each time I come close to giving up a wave splashes me in the face, shaking the thought out of my head and urging me on. It feels like the waves are playing a game with me, like when Baba and I wrestle. I would scream and pretend that he was hurting me and ask him to stop being cruel, but when he stopped I would poke him again and goad him on.

As I negotiate whether or not to give up, a huge wave picks me up. As I come down I feel that the sea has turned into a monster with a huge, greedy mouth. The monster gobbles me up and I fall deeper and deeper into his dark monstrous belly.

I slowly fall into darkness ...

The Morpheus

Morpheus in Greek mythology is a God of dreams and nightmares. He appears in different human forms.

My eyes are twitching; I can see light from under my eyelids. I want to open them, but I can't. My eyelids feel very heavy. My head feels heavy too. My whole body feels numb. At first I think I am at home and expect to hear Maman coming into my room and waking me up with her kisses and funny singing. She always sings something about a lazy boy she loves and tells me: I'd better get my lazy bottom out of that bed and get ready for school because it is a beautiful morning. It didn't matter if it was sunny or pouring cats and dogs, Maman always said it was a beautiful morning.

Trying to lift my head and see why Maman is not there, a sharp pain stabs my head and I feel very sick. What is wrong with me? Am I ill? Then I remember everything, the terrible night, the dinghy, the roaring sea and the monster that swallowed Rexi and myself and maybe everybody else. I can even taste the salty sea water in my throat, but why does it feel warm and nice? Maybe the monster hasn't yet eaten me. Maybe he had enough food for one night that he decided to take me to his food storage and keep me there for later. I heard of some hidden cities under the sea, maybe that is where I am right now. I have to open my eyes and see for myself.

I force myself to open my eyes a little bit, but the light is too strong and I quickly close them again and try to listen carefully to find out what is going on. I hear people walking and talking around me. I can't understand anything they are saying, they all sound like mumbles to me and there is not a familiar voice I recognise. A warm hand touches my forehead and a few words are said in a soft voice. I have to open my eyes and this time I manage to keep them open enough to see a smiling face bent over me and talking to me. I open my mouth to ask where I am and where are Maman and Baba, but my throat hurts like it has been cut to pieces. I feel too tired to try again, so I just close my eyes again and go back to sleep.

In my dreams I see my grandparents, my friends and my Uncle Roozbeh, who is giving me a ride on his motorbike. We twist our way between the cars and they honk their horns at us. Some put their heads out of the window and shout at Uncle Roozbeh for being so foolish and driving so crazy. One of the cars honks its horn so loudly that it hurts my ears and I wake up with a shriek.

'Maman, Baba… Maman…' I shout, But only a strange sound comes out of my mouth. I don't know where I am. I am scared, in pain and I want my parents. A woman with long hair and glasses comes running to my side and says something that I cannot understand.

'Where are my Maman and Baba?' I open my mouth to ask her, again nothing comes out. I am ready to burst into tears.

She says something again, I don't know what she is saying, but I can see that she is smiling and she doesn't want to hurt me. I look around myself and see lots of people in the other beds. Some of them are still asleep, some have masks on their faces and some have needles in their arms. In the far corner of the room I see Mahsa and Mehrdad's mum sitting up in bed and crying. When she sees me looking at her she waves to me and says something and cries even more. I can't see my parents anywhere. What if the sea has swallowed them? What if they never come back to me? I start shaking and crying.

The lady in glasses (I think she is a nurse), puts her arms around my shoulders and says something in a soft voice. I guess she is trying to make me feel better. I want to ask her if she has seen my parents, but I can't say anything. No words come out. She gives me a glass of water to drink and helps me sit up in my bed. The water stings my tongue and my throat, I feel funny in my tummy and the room spins around my head. Waking up is not fun, I want to go back to sleep and feel nothing.

I am in and out of dreams again. This time I dream I am in my own room. My friend Sina is there too. We are playing dinosaur attack. This is a new game Sina and I have made up a few weeks ago. First we build some houses with building blocks and make roads with cars driving everywhere, then the dinosaurs come stomping, and romping and crash into the buildings, sending blocks everywhere and turning cars over. Rexi loves this game and, being the king he is always at the lead of the other dinosaurs. Sina and I laugh and laugh as we rebuild the houses and tell the dinosaurs off.

Just then Sheerin comes through the door, clutching her dolly to her chest and tells Rexi it is time to go. I get angry as I see Rexi following her and say Rexi is mine and we are in the middle of a good game. The two of them just shake their heads and go out of the room, leaving me screaming at the top of my voice….

Nurses come running to comfort me. They change my wet pyjamas and bed (how embarrassing!). I can't stop shaking and crying. They check my temperature, give me more medicine and try to feed me, which proves a mistake because my stomach rejects food and I bring up everything within minutes. Unhappy about being awake and too tired, I go back to sleep.

Am I dreaming again? I hear Maman and Baba talking. Feel their hands in mine. Even smell that special Maman and Baba smell. Not wanting to lose them again I keep my eyes closed and listen to them.

'Look at her, she is still holding on to her little dolly. I feel for her poor mum and dad. They must be totally destroyed. How proud they were of their beautiful talented little girl.'

'I hadn't realised they were alive?'

'Yes. They are both strong athletes remember? But what is that life worth?'

Oh, no, not another horrible dream. I force my

eyes open. Surprisingly my eyelids are light as feathers and the lights no longer bother me. Maman and Baba are looking at a newspaper across my bed. I see a flash of a pink top and black hair on the page and try to sit up to have a better look. The child on the page is stretched out on the sand. black hair spreads all over the white sand making a contrasting image. Her big eyes are shut and there is a faint smile on the corner of her mouth. Dolly safely nestling in her arms. Her feet still under the sand and her flowery pink top has turned green overnight. I try to reach the newspaper to have a better look. Maman and Baba notice that I am awake and quickly put the newspaper away to reach for my hands. They sit either side of my bed holding my hands and shower me with kisses. I must have slept for a long time because Baba's beard has grown and they both look older.

I look at Maman and Baba and cry. I want to tell them about my dream. I want to ask them, where have they been. How did they find me? How long have I been here? I open my mouth, to try to talk but I can't say a word. What is happening to me? Why can't I talk?

'Don't worry son, you are safe now.' I hear my Baba telling me. 'You have been very brave and strong. The rescue team told us that you have swam a long distance in the rough sea. They all think you have done a great job of it. Maman and I are very proud of you. Just wait till I tell your Uncle Sohrab, you know what he will say? He will say,

I told you that boy has our blood running in him.' Baba tries to laugh but there are tears in his voice and I can see from his eyes that he is very sad. Both Maman and he have been crying. Their eyes are red and they look tired and ugly.

With a lot of hand and face and head movements, which I find exhausting, I make them understand that I want to know if Rexi has been rescued too.

'No, he must have swum to the other side of the sea by the time the rescue team got to us. You know how fast T-Rexes swim. Maybe he has found an island full of dinosaurs and is making lots of new friends by now.'

I'm not happy with the idea of Rexi finding other friends on a faraway island. He is my friend and I want him to come back to me. But I am too tired to argue.

Maman and Baba sit next to my bed all night and most of the next day. They tell me how Baba was trying to find Maman and me in the sea. They found others and helped them get to the rescue boats. He refused to get into the boat himself as he wanted to search for us. He continued swimming all night until exhaustion took over. His unconscious body eventually washed up on the shore. He was transferred to hospital.

Maman, who had been treated by the local medical team, had looked everywhere for Baba and me.

'I was worried sick. I went from one tent to the

other asking people if they had seen either of you. I went to the shore where the unlucky ones were laid out and could not find you two there. I cried and begged the rescue team for any signs. They told me about Baba refusing to get on the boat and suggested that maybe I should come to this hospital in Mytilene because some people with more serious injuries had been transferred here. I had to beg the bus driver to let me on the bus to travel to the Island's capital.' tears stream down her face as she tells me this. She kisses my hand over and over rubbing lots of tears and bogies all over it.

Mahsa and Mehrdad's mum is not in the hospital anymore. Maman says they have to continue on their journey to Sweden where they plan to join their relatives. She says Mahsa and Mehrdad are ok but the way she says it doesn't convince me. Maman and Baba don't mention Sheerin at all.

While Baba snoozes with his head on my bed, Maman tells me stories including my favourite, the Rolling Pumpkin:

"... *Faster and faster down the winding steep hill went the huge rolling pumpkin. The old lady felt dizzy and worried. What if the other wild animals find her too and what if they didn't let her go. Her fears were confirmed when not much longer down the hill her pumpkin was stopped by another powerful paw.*

"Tell me rolling pumpkin, have you seen an old lady?" The tiger roared as he asked this.

"No." said the old lady inside the pumpkin "No, I swear to the gods of the fairies and all the feathered birds that I have not seen an old lady. Now could you please give me a push so I can carry on rolling down the hill."

The tiger was not convinced. He kept his powerful paw on the pumpkin a bit longer and examined the pumpkin all around. But he could not find anything and could see no use keeping a useless pumpkin any longer. So he gave it a mighty push and the pumpkin rolled even faster down the winding road …"

The nurses and doctors in the hospital are very kind to me. They look after me and give me food and warm clothes and colouring books and pens. One of the nurses has found an old dinosaur toy which belonged to her son when he was little and brought it to me. She must have heard about Rexi and how I loved dinosaurs. It is a long necked, purplish Brachiosaurus, like the one I had back home. I thank the lady and put the dinosaur on the table next to my bed.

'Don't you want to play with your new dinosaur?' Maman asks me, about an hour later when she notices I have not touched it at all.

I just shake my head. I don't feel like playing with the dinosaur. It even makes me sad each time I look at it.

When I am well enough, they release me from the hospital. By then everybody else has gone. How about Sheerin? I make my parents understand that I want to know what happened to her. My parents mumble a few words and quickly change the subject. I know by the way they look at each other and the way Maman's eyes fill with tears that something must have happened to Sheerin. What I had seen in the newspaper must have been real, not a dream. The sea must have gobbled her up too. I was sad. Sheerin was my friend and despite being a girl she was still very fun to play with. We had lots of fun singing and making up silly games in the past few weeks we had travelled together. It isn't fair. Nothing is fair.

The doctor tells Maman and Baba (Maman who speaks some English translates it to Baba and me) that I will eventually find my speech.

'It's just the shock; you must understand that this young man has been through a lot. You all have but it usually hits the children a lot harder. But he is young and resilient and will heal as time passes.'

He then pats me on the shoulder and wishes me good luck. Baba and Maman have bought chocolate for the nurses and doctors to say thank you to them all.

Outside the hospital it is sunny and bright. The sea is calm and beautiful almost as beautiful as the sea near old Maman's house. I cannot believe that this is the same angry and horrible sea that almost gobbled me up. I imagine that the monster sleeping somewhere under that blue sea and waiting for the night to wake up and hunt little girls and boys and their toys.

'Let's go to the beach and have an ice cream before we leave.' Baba suggests knowing how much I love eating an ice cream on the beach.

But I pull my hand out of his and shake my head to show them I don't want to. I don't want to go anywhere near the sea.

'But it is ok sweetie you are safe and we are not going on a boat again. We just want to sit down on the beach and eat ice cream.' Maman says bending down to look into my eyes.

I start to cry and shake all over. I want to scream and run away.

'It is ok baby. We don't need to go to the beach we can have our ice cream in town.' Maman hugs me tight and kisses my tears away. Baba puts his arm around my shoulder and gently walks me away from the sea and towards the town centre.

There are lots of people sitting or sleeping on the benches and on the pavements. Some gather in big noisy groups and talk at the top of their voices. Baba says they are refugees like us, trying to find a way to continue their journeys to Europe. He says that local people are not happy about all these foreigners taking over their streets and making the city look so ugly.

'But there are lots who feel sympathy for the

refugees and they have set up rescue and medical centres to help those in need.

'I heard there was a restaurant owner in Lesbos who had set up a campsite behind her restaurant for refugees and gave them food too.' Maman says as she makes a de tour to avoid stepping on a sleeping man on the pavement.

We are going to meet the agent who is supposed to help us with the rest of our journey. Baba says he has spoken with Matilda's father on the phone and reproached him for putting us in such a danger.

'I told him we were disappointed and very upset by the way things have been dealt with, after all we paid him a lot of hard found money to be safe and travel in peace. He said Roozbeh had already talked to him and he was really sorry to hear about our misfortune. He promised to make it up to us and said his agent will come and take us to Italy from where we could fly to England.'

Uncle Roozbeh has sent us some money over. When we get to Athens we manage to buy some new clothes and a suitcase. Maman and Baba want to buy me a new T-Rex but I shake my head and refuse to buy it. I almost cry. The dinosaur they want to buy me, looks so much like Rexi, but it is not Rexi and it makes me so sad. Maman and Baba end up arguing and blaming each other for upsetting me. Maman cries because Baba tells her it was all her fault. If it wasn't for her and her stupid activities none of us had to go through this. I have never seen my parents talk to each other like that. I hate to see them that way.

'Look, we are approaching our new home. This is England.' Maman says bending over me and pointing at the tiny airplane window. Down there the bright sunlight makes the sea sparkle like there are a million little crystals floating on its surface. A curving white coastline slithers like a snake drawing a clear border between the sea and the land which is green as far as the eye can see.

'Isn't it beautiful?' She turns to Baba inviting him to have a look. Baba smiles and nods in silence. He holds Maman's hand and rests his head on her shoulder to have a better look.

'We made it. We are safe now.' Maman says. I am looking through the window but can hear the tears in her voice.

Looking down at the square fields I smile and think 'our new home is certainly very green.'

The Dragon

A large lizard or serpent like creature conceived in some traditions as evil while in others, known as beneficent.

The only two windows in the little room at the airport are nothing but two big pieces of thick glass. We can only see the security people sitting in their office swivelling in their chairs or staring at their computers. I can't hear what they are saying as the glass between us is very thick, but I can see that every now and again the kind fat man who gave me hot chocolate makes a joke and the others laugh.

Sometimes when he sees me looking, he waves at me and smiles. He says something to the others and they all look at me briefly and swivel back to their computers. The kind fat man points to the bowls of fruit and biscuits and crisps on the window and tells me I am allowed to eat as much as I like. The ones with jam and cream between them are my favourite, but Maman's face tells me that she is not happy with me eating too many of those.

There is a television screen quite high up on the wall. Baba manages to find me a kid's channel to keep me busy as there isn't much else to do and we don't know how long we will be kept here. I like sitting on the big, red, leather bean bag in the middle of the room. It is funny the way it changes shape as I move around. It makes a hole in the middle when I jump high up.

My parents tell me off when I jump too much. They clearly are not in the mood to entertain my craziness. Maman is nervously pacing the tiny space between the locked door and the toilet on the other side of the room. Baba is lying down on a reclining chair on the other side of the room pretending to be asleep. They have been told that when an interpreter arrives they will have to be interviewed. I wonder what an interview is and why my parents are so worried about it.

'Ok, let's go through it all before we are called for the interview.' Maman says as she stops in front of Baba's chair rubbing her hands on the side of her trousers as if she is trying to wipe them clean.

Baba slowly opens his eyes and looks at her. I can see he wants to be left alone, to go back to pretending to be asleep. But Maman doesn't want to leave him alone.

'We have already been through all that several times, why do we need to do it again?' Baba protests, knowing too well that he has no choice but to listen to Maman.

'We cannot afford to have any discrepancies in our stories. If we want them to believe us we have to match word for word.'

I want to know what discrepancy means, but having lost my voice, I can't ask and carry on pretending that I am watching Teletubbies as I listen to them.

'You just tell them that you had to leave because of me. Hopefully they won't be asking you too many questions.'

'I certainly will be more than happy to tell them that we are all in this mess because of you.' Baba snorts.

I quietly nod. I too have been blaming Maman for getting us into trouble.

'Well, I am sorry that you have forgotten how passionate and supportive you used to be about my activities. But right now being bitter about it and blaming me does not help us in any way. We need to focus on our future. We will have plenty of time to deal with the past later.'

I can hear the tears in Maman's voice and feel sorry for her. I get up from my bean bag and go to give her a hug to show her that I am not very angry with her for putting us all through this stupid adventure. I don't want Maman to cry all the time but my hug makes her cry even more.

The immigration officer who comes to take Maman for her interview looks like a grumpy bulldog. His cheeks hang all the way to his chest mixing halfway with many layers of chin. His eyes are only half open. I think he prefers to keep them totally closed. Through the buttons of his stretched navy uniform I can see his hairy belly poking out. My eyes catch and stay fixed on the walkie-talkie on the side of his arm. It crackles every few seconds and I know I would give anything to have one of those. He gives me a sleepy look and tries to smile only to give it up immediately as if finding it too much.

'Maryam Farahani and Siavash Bakhshi' He says looking at the file in his hand and pronouncing my parents' names slowly and in a funny way.

Baba jumps up to his feet and Maman half runs to the door.

'We are going to do your interviews now. Can you please come with me?' the lady who is standing next to the officer translates in Farsi.

'Which one of us first?' Maman asks.

'If you could both go with me to establish a few things, then we decide who goes first.'

I go and hold Maman's hand. I don't want to be left alone in that room. Maman understands how I feel and pleads with the officer. 'Can we bring him with us?'

'No, he can stay here. We can't take children to interview rooms.'

Panicking that I am going to be left alone in this strange place with people I don't even understand, I suddenly let out a shrill scream which surprises me and everybody else. The bulldog's eyes shoot open to their full size, showing a pale blue marble like colour and dull bluish whites splattered with red stripes. The kind fat man who has been half sitting half lying on his chair springs to his feet with an amazing speed that is unbelievable for his size and the lady who is watching her screen swivels her chair and looks at me in amazement.

'I am so sorry sir.' Says Maman after recovering from her shock 'He has been through a hell of a lot and is very sensitive right now.' she explains squeezing my shoulder gently.

'Oh, ok then. Tell me are you both going to apply for asylum in your own rights or is one of you going to be dependent on the other?' His eyes have gone back to their original sleepy position and I feel his annoyance.

Maman steps forward and explains that Baba and I are only here because of her.

'Ok then. You come with me first.' The officer turns around and walks away expecting Maman and the other lady to follow him, which they do.

Maman is away at her interview for a long time. I can see Baba looking at the window every so often waiting

73

for her to come back. I pretend I am busy trying to figure out a puzzle but can't help copying Baba and looking at the window. When she finally comes back she looks very tired and I can see she has been crying again. The officer stands in the door and asks me if I have had any lunch. I shake my head surprised that he is paying any attention to me.

'He has been eating biscuits and crisps. He doesn't like the food they give us.' Baba tells him. The food they give us for lunch time smells and tastes funny. Maman and Baba hardly touch it either.

'I don't blame him, that food is awful. Isn't there anything else you could give him?'

He asks the kind fat man and his team.

'We can get him a sandwich.'

'Do you like McDonalds? They can get you a happy meal if you want to.' Wow. Maman must have said something in her interview to make the bulldog interested in me. I only had McDonalds twice when we were in Italy and I loved it.

'He may look grumpy but he is a good man. He is only doing his job.' Maman says to me when the bulldog has taken Baba away for his interview.

'Shall I help you with that puzzle?'

Maman sits down next to me and picks up a random piece. I look at her wanting to know what the interview was like. She reads my look and tells me the immigration officer wanted to know who we were and why we have left our country to come here.

'They want to make sure people who come here are good people. They don't want trouble.'

If I could speak I would have asked her what they meant by trouble and how would they know if we make trouble. My old head teacher Mrs Zakeri used to call me a troublemaker, even when somebody else had picked the fight or broken something, I always got the blame. 'Don't go looking for trouble.' My grandparents would advise me as I went out to play.

'Don't end up in any trouble.' my parents would tell me when they sent me off to a birthday party or a sleepover.

What Maman says worries me a lot. What if I end up in trouble at my English school? What if their head teacher thinks I am a troublemaker? Will the bulldog come and take me away from my parents? I feel something hard in my chest. How I wish I could talk and let my Maman know how I feel. Instead I throw myself into her arms and hold her tightly and quietly tell myself I am going to be extra good and try not to get into any trouble at school.

We only have to wait another few hours in that tiny room before they find us somewhere to live and send us away. While I happily feast on my chicken nuggets and fries my parents tell each other about their interviews and what they each have said in their replies to the questions.

***

'My perfect little boy is broken Agha Joon and it is all my fault.' Maman sobs.

'But it is, even Siavash seems to think this was all my fault. He can't stand me anymore, keeps himself out of the house most of the time.'

Why is she saying I am broken? I check myself over. Looking at my hands and wiggling my toes and blinking my eyes, everything seems to be working fine. When something is broken it doesn't work anymore, like when Agha Joon's DVD player was broken (by me), it made funny crackling noises and would not show the films anymore. Or when Maman's mobile phone was damaged (I accidentally dropped in the toilet), I couldn't play any games on it and she couldn't call her work.

Agha Reza's big expensive car was not really broken or damaged when I played monster truck on it. A few scratches and dents don't damage a car, it could still go as fast as before. But Agha Reza said it was damaged and made such a fuss that my Baba had to give him a lot of money.

'I miss the little chatterbox boy he used to be.' Maman said sniffing.

Funny she is saying this. Has she forgotten telling me off for talking when she was on the phone or working on her computer? Agha Joon must have asked her the same question because she gives a wet laugh and says, 'Yes, I know what a fool I was. My friends have been asking us to go and visit them in London, but we can't. Not with him wetting his bed every night.'

76

Why does she have to tell Maman Bozorg and Agha Joon all those embarrassing things? It is not my fault that I wet my bed. It is Rexi telling me to do it. When I need to wee Rexi just laughs and tells me under the sea it is ok to be naughty and wee anywhere. He pees in the sea too and his wee is so much that it makes a big wave and all the fish and mermaids and I, we all jump on it. It is such good fun. But then I wake up and find myself shivering in my wet Pyjamas. I try to cover my wet bed and change the wet pyjamas before Maman and Baba find out. But they always find out anyway and things get worse.

'Get him some nappies' Baba says leaning against my bedroom door with half open puffy eyes.

'No, He is almost eight. There are no nappies for that age. We should try to help him get better.'

'He is not getting better and we can't afford to buy more bedding.'

'You can help by getting up once in a while and taking him to the toilet instead of drowning yourself in that horrible drink' Maman hisses at him.

'I do what I like. This is a free country.' He turns around and leaves Maman ripping the bedcovers away and pulling at my wet pyjamas violently.

Times like that I see little of my own Maman in her. I don't like this wet eyed, angry person who takes her anger out on me and acts as if it is all my fault. I miss my old, lovely parents who hardly ever quarrelled and if they did they would soon make up and laugh and dance together.

Sometimes they don't even look like their old selves. Maman has lost weight and looks skinnier than ever. Her hair is no longer shiny and there are purple rings around her eyes. She doesn't wear any makeup and sometimes her skin looks grey instead of the lovely peach it used to be. Baba has become fat and looks a lot older than before. He has huge bags under his eyes and hardly ever smiles anymore. I don't want to hug him because his stubble scratches my face and he smells funny.

'The doctors say he will eventually get better. But oh, Agha Joon, it is heart breaking to see him like this.' Sniff, sniff, sob sob, I tiptoe down the stairs and hug Maman trying to make her feel better. I expect her to turn around and tell me off for being out of bed, but she gently pats my hair.

'Do you want to talk to Agha Joon Azizam?' and she put the phone next to my ear before I have a chance to reply.

'Salam my lovely son. How are you? Have you become English yet?' Agha Joon's voice is very far away. I want him to be there and hug me. I miss him and I miss Maman Bozorg too.

'So, your Maman tells me you have joined the football team in your school. Show them how it is done will you?' He chuckles. I only nod.

'Here Maman Bozorg wants to talk to you.'

"Asale man, Gole man, Omid man," like she

78

always calls me my honey, my flower, my hope and tells me how much she misses me and how much she loves me and how she has kept all my toys safe for me. I listen and smile and nod and then give the phone back to Maman who says goodbye to them and comes with me upstairs. She lies down on my bed and hugs me tightly.

'Uncle Roozbeh was very impressed when I told him about your football team.'

I am proud of myself too. At first I was worried that nobody would pick me on their side to play football. Our PE teacher made sure I'd get picked. I made some huge mistakes because I couldn't understand what people were shouting about and didn't exactly know who was in my team.

'Pass it to Harry, come on pass it to Harry.'

Not quite sure who Harry was, I passed the ball to a blond boy on my right who I realised by the angry shouts of my teammates, played on the opposing team. Yet by the end of the game, I had made myself a few friends. My football is not the best. Sina and Parviz and Mehran all played better than me, but I was fast and didn't mind getting under other people's feet to sneak the ball out. Our opposing teams always called me a cheat and demanded a penalty. Sometimes the referees would give me a yellow or red card. It was still fun and worth it as I usually got the ball back to our side of the field.

Starting school has been very exciting and scary too. I didn't know a single person and didn't understand what they were saying. I was taken to the classroom on

Monday and our teacher Miss Chapman introduced me to the class and asked them to say hello to me.

'Hello Omid'. They all say some waving to me. I wave back and try to smile. I look at the door to make sure it is still there in case I need to run away and go home.

I have been wanting to go to school very much. I was bored at home doing nothing and listening to my parents argue all the time. But now that school is real and I am facing all these grinning boys and girls, I get really scared and I'm not sure I want to stay.

Miss Chapman points to a little girl and says something to her. Maman translates.

'That little girl is Zari. Her parents are from Afghanistan. She speaks a little Farsi and she is going to help you find your way around the school.'

Zari is not the only girl in the class. There are as many girls as boys. They don't have to go to different schools here. I am told to go and sit next to Zari and Alfie who is a chubby little boy with eyes as blue as the sky and lashes so white they are almost invisible.

I was year two, when I was in Iran but here people start school very young and they put me in year three. Maman tells me that if I had been born in August instead of November, I would have to go straight to year four. Imagine jumping two years at a time. Baba was not happy.

'It is going to be hard on this poor child. He has to learn the language as well as catching up with the year he hasn't done.'

'Omid is a clever boy. He will learn very quickly. In this country they don't have exams for early years. They only place children according to their ages.'

What if Maman is not right and I become the most stupid child in the class? What if nobody wants to be friends with me?

'I told him that at first nobody wanted to pick you for their team because they thought you could not play. Now everyone wants you to play for them.' Maman giggles a bit and gives me a good squeeze. Then she tells me the story of the Rolling Pumpkin to help me go to sleep.

'... *The pumpkin rolled faster and faster through the winding steep road. The old woman sensed that she was getting closer to her home and hoped that she wouldn't have any more unpleasant encounters. But suddenly another powerful paw stopped the pumpkin.*

"You, rolling Pumpkin, have you seen an old woman anywhere around?" hissed the big bad wolf.

"No, I haven't seen anyone." said the old woman trying to change her voice as much as she could so the big bad wolf wouldn't recognize her.

"I swear on the kings of fairies and all the sweetness of fruit and berries, I have not seen an old woman anywhere. Now, can you please give me a push and set me on my way

81

again?"

The big bad wolf was not very convinced and started to sniff around the pumpkin. His eyes could not see anything but his nose told him that there was something inside that pumpkin and he tried to get it out. The old lady was horrified and gathering all her powers she pushed the pumpkin forward and managed to get away from the wolf's clutches. The pumpkin went faster and faster and the wolf ran faster after it. At the front gate of the old lady the pumpkin stopped and she came out and managed to unlock her door and get into her house just as the wolf reached the threshold. The big bad wolf stood there huffing and puffing for a while but at the end, he gave up and went back to the forest and the old woman was safe at last.'

The Unicorn

The Unicorn is a legendary mythological animal resembling a horse with a single horn. It symbolizes purity and can even be known to help heal some diseases.

'Hello Omid. My name is Nina. I am an art therapist.' She puts her hands on her knees and bends down to look at me. Her nails are coloured green. I like them. Maman used to paint her nails different colours when we were still in Iran and she was happy.

'You know what an art therapist is?'

I shake my head. I had only heard Maman and Baba talking about it when I was watching Octonauts. The Octonauts live in an Octopod under the sea. They go exploring the sea and rescuing sea creatures that are injured or trapped. Isn't that cool? I've decided I want to be an Octonaut when I grow up. In an Octopod even the meanest and angriest of sea monsters can't hurt me.

'I had a meeting with the headmistress of the school today.' Maman was saying after dinner a few days ago. I knew how to listen to her with one ear and still get to hear the program I was watching with the other. I had done that before. It worked easy peasy.

'What was it all about this time?' Baba said not sounding very interested. He was puffing on an e-cigarette these days because Maman wouldn't allow him to smoke real cigarettes inside the house.

'The school has found an art therapist to help Omid.'

'What is an art therapist? Do they even know what they are doing? Last time they suggested speech therapy.'

'Speech therapy is for correcting speech and Omid has none at the moment to be corrected. Art therapy is more to let him express his feelings through painting and drawing and it might help him overcome his trauma. Nina the art therapist is actually half Iranian and can speak Farsi which is good for Omid with his limited English.'

'Your teacher tells me you are very good at painting. Let's go to the art room and do some painting shall we?' Nina's Farsi is funny. Uncle Roozbeh would have laughed if he were here.

I had been to the art room before. I love the smell of paint in there and the way all the walls are covered with paintings of flowers, animals, dragons and superheroes. One of my dinosaur paintings is there too..

'These paintings are all done by the children. Aren't they amazing?'

I nod politely and continue to look. There is a painting of a little girl with shiny black hair sitting on a small boat with her dog. She reminds me of Sheerin. I stand there looking at her. I want to paint Sheerin.

Nina is busy bringing out pots of different coloured paint and brushes and paper.

'So what do you want to paint?'

I just shrug.

'Here, let's try,' she pushes a big, thick piece of paper and some brushes towards me and opens the pots of paint. She starts on her own piece without waiting for me.

I pick up the brush and dip it into the black, shiny paint and try to paint Sheerin's long, black hair. It comes out messy and ugly. I get angry and splash black paint all over it and stab the paper with the brush.

'I can do that too.' Nina says with a smile. She takes her brush and stubs red paint all over her painting.

After messing around for a while, Nina says we should try and paint something else. This time I paint myself as an Octonaut riding in Gup A, exploring the sea.

'That is amazing. Is that you? I like Octonauts too. I watch them sometimes with my little brother.'

I hadn't seen any grown-ups that liked watching Octonauts.

'You really need a big headlight to go into that dark sea don't you?' She points to the part of the sea I had painted black. She didn't ask why I had painted the sea black. Others always make such a fuss over that. 'Blue dear, blue' they say. 'The sea is blue.' No it isn't. I want to tell them. Instead I keep quiet and carry-on spreading darkness over my paper. Nina gives me an idea. Maybe if I paint myself a big head light I can go into that dark part of the sea and look for Rexi and Sheerin.

The Pumpkin

The rolling Pumpkin is a folkloric story about an old woman who finds safety in a giant pumpkin.

I am sitting at the upper deck of the bus. We are in London and double decker buses are my favourite. I have been forcing Baba and his friend Agha Miran on and off them all day long. When you sit up there in the front row, it feels like you are the driver and can turn the bus this way and that. Maman is in a conference. She has been invited to talk about children in Iran, Baba and I have a whole day to roam London. We have already been to the Eye. I didn't

87

like it much. It is veerrrry sloooow. And we have had lunch at a good Iranian restaurant. Baba wanted to visit them and see if they need a chef. Him and the owner had a long talk about opening an Iranian restaurant in Leeds, while I had my Chelo kebab. Baba is smiling again.

'Shall we go and see the big dinosaurs at the Natural History museum?' Agha Miran asks. I think he is bored of getting off and on the buses. I shake my head. I don't want to see dinosaurs. I want to sit on the bus and look at the very slow traffic of London. It reminds me of my bus rides in Tehran, when Maman Bozorg and I went to see her older sister in downtown Tehran. Khanomi had a big wooden chest with yummy things in it. I liked her Lawashak. Nobody can make Lawashak like Khanomi. The ones Baba bought me from the Iranian shop today taste nothing like hers. The wrappings have pictures of different fruits on them but they all taste the same. Khanomi's plum lawashak tastes exactly like plum and her peach tastes just like a yummy, ripe peach.

'We are going to meet your Maman and Khaleh Sepi in an hour. Khaleh Sepi has got us all tickets to go to London Zoo. They have a Halloween show there tonight. How fun is that?' I like it when he sounds like my old Baba.

Khaleh Sepi is Maman's friend. She has already visited us in Leeds and brought me a huge Octopod toy. I love playing with Captain Barnacles and Kwazi. Sometimes I wear my eye patch and pretend to be Kwazi. He is the funniest of all the Octonauts.

The Zoo is full of light and there are people dressed as ghosts and vampires and witches. Spiders and bats are hanging from every corner, even the animals seem to be excited about something. Pumpkins with carved eyes and toothy mouths are everywhere. The gorillas are the happiest. I watch them. A huge one takes a chunky bit from one of the pumpkins and throws it around to his friend who does the same and passes it on to the next. The lioness is surprised to find a big yellow head perching atop of her favourite rock. She examines it carefully and throws it around with a powerful paw strike. Sniffing the seedy insides of the broken pumpkin the lioness shakes her big head and walks away angry.

I laugh and look around to see how the tigers and wolves react when they find no old women inside their pumpkins. Wolves and tigers are nowhere to be seen. A few yards away a giraffe is munching on the leaves that poke out of his pumpkin's eyes and mouth. The Penguins just stand there looking the other way, ignoring the freezing pumpkins that have been placed on their icy platforms.

Still looking for wolves and tigers, my eyes fall on a big, see-through pumpkin rolling around in between the cages. A man wearing a skeleton costume is inside it and rolls around with his hands and his legs. It is enormous, with huge eyes that look like lighted windows and a big mouth that looks like a dark cave.

'Nigah Maman, kadoo qelqelizan.' I am shocked to hear my own voice. The grown-ups who up to that point had been chatting non-stop, now look at me with their mouths open and their eyes big.

'Maman, Baba look, a rolling pumpkin.' I repeat

89

and point to the pumpkin that is coming closer. Maman and Baba both crouch down and take my hands and look into my mouth. It looks like it is their turn to lose their voice.

'Can we please face time Maman Bozorg?' I ask excited. I want to show her the big rolling pumpkin.

'Of course you can my darling.' Maman says after a long pause. Her eyes are still on my mouth but now they are filling up with tears again. She takes her mobile phone in her pocket and scrolls down names looking for Maman Bozorg, while Baba is holding me tight and crying softly into my neck.

'Maman Bozorg, look I have found a big rolling pumpkin. Now you can come to visit us. We can put you in there and even in the zoo, no one can hurt you.'

'How clever of you Azizam. Now I must come and visit. Oh, I am so excited.'

'There is a lioness here but I still haven't found the tiger and the wolf.'

'Take a photo of that pumpkin so we can show it to Uncle Roozbeh when he comes home.'

Khaleh Sepi has already stopped the rolling pumpkin and brings it towards us. The man in skeleton costume says hello and poses for a photo with me.

'Can we print this photo Maman? I want to show it to my class Monday morning during show and tell session.' I look up at Maman and Baba who are holding hands and nodding through tears.

An extract from Mina's second book in this trilogy due for release ... 2023

Omid saw them huddled around a computer screen in the library. They were absorbed in something on the screen and by the look of it, it was not one of those funny memes they always found on the TikTok or YouTube. He could hear the booming voice of Harry B who as usual could not keep it down, even in a library.

'Well, let that be a good lesson to the rest of them. See if they still dare to cross our channel.' He was saying, pointing at the screen. Katie Moor said something in her usual, soft, inaudible whisper, to which Harry replied with impatient ringing in his tone.

'Safety? What do you mean safety? Why didn't they stay in France then? Are you telling me France is a dictatorship?' Harry looked around at others, seeking support. Joshua and Dylan shook their heads asserting disagreement, while Denisha pretended she was reading the captions.

'It was expected anyway, my dad has been saying all along, that it will happen sooner or later. This is the busiest channel after all.' Joshua said matter of fact.

'They should have more sense than getting in such a tiny, unsafe dinghy.'

'It's not as if they had many choices.'

'Stop pretending that they had no choice. They could stay in France, or Italy or several other European countries.'

'So why do you think they risk their lives to come here?'

'They know we're softies, that's why. They know they can milk our welfare system, that's why.'

'You are a heartless jerk Harry, that's what.'

'Ok Mother Theresa, how do you suggest we house and feed all these people?' from where he was standing Omid could see Harry's ears turning red.

'Our war heroes, ex- soldiers, sleep on the street, my older brother still shares a room with me, and He can't afford renting a private room. My cousin must pay half his earning towards his rent because he cannot get council accommodation, you know why? because those asylum seekers have priority. They get all the available council houses, and their rent is paid for them. How is that fair?'

'Have any of you visited Omid's family recently? Aren't they doing well? When they arrived in this country a few years ago, they could not even afford to buy a spare pair of pants for their son, who if you all remember well had a habit of wetting himself.' Harry looked up and froze. He hadn't noticed Omid standing there listening. Their gaze met for a few seconds and as if to set himself a challenge he continued 'They have bought a nice house and a fancy car whiles my parent struggle to pay their bills, why? Because nobody cares about British people. Because good hearted people like our Katie here, weep for them not for us.' Grinding his teeth he lowered his gaze, he slumped back into his chair and swirled around to look at the screen.

Omid, overwhelmed with rage and grief, did not say a word; he just stood there looking confused and forlorn. He was struggling with different emotions. He knew opening his mouth would be very risky as his eyes tingled and tears threatened to flow. The last thing he wanted was for his friends to see him cry. He pretended he was looking at the screen over Harry's shoulder. As always, it was Katie and Dylan and others who stood up to Harry and shut him up.

'You are an asshole Harry'.

'Have you no shame man? That family have treated you like a son.'

'His parents work hard; they are both skilled people.'

'It's not their fault that your parents are poor...'

'You are a thick-headed racist, that's what you are.'

Omid quietly turned around and left the library. He needed to get away, to be alone, to process his feelings. His friend's probably thought him a coward, running away when he should have smashed Harry's face for insulting his family. Of course he knew they were right. He was a coward. How else could he explain putting up with Harry and even laugh at his racist jokes? It was not like he could claim he had not noticed Harry's racist attitudes. His whole social media was reeking of them.

Sitting in a quiet corner of the café, he took his

phone out and looked up the latest news. The family that had drowned last night had a little girl around the same age as Sheerin. There were no pictures of them out yet but Omid had a feeling that she too had black shiny hair and maybe had a dolly that went down with her.

'Things must be pretty desperate back home to make people put their children in those dinghies.' Katie sat quietly beside him on the couch looking at the screen of the mobile phone over his shoulder. He hadn't noticed her coming in.

'I am really ashamed for not standing up to Harry.'

'He is the one who should be ashamed for saying those things.'

'Yes, but I have put up with him, haven't I. You guys have always stood up to him while I just laughed at his stupid jokes and let him be' Anger was boiling in him.

'It's in your nature to give people a chance.' She was being particularly tender with him. 'you had a hard time fitting in Omid. You needed friends to replace what you had lost when you came here. We were all hoping that mixing with your kind family would make Harry see foreigners in a different light.' Omid was surprised how insightful Katie was. She was known to be kind-hearted but being this thoughtful and smart was a new discovery to him. He took his eyes of the screen and looked Katie in the eyes. Her eyes were of a deep, clear blue, the colour of the sea when it was calm and peaceful. Suddenly he longed to dive into those depths and let the warmth of it engulf him.

Acknowledgments

Omid, the young hero of this story may simply be a fictional character, but he is very much real and lives in too many refugee children I have met through my work over the years. Uprooted, displaced children traumatized by horrific experiences from their past. who desperately try to 'fit in' and come to terms with their new reality. In the majority of cases, schools and local authorities are not well informed. More often than not they lack enough resources to adequately provide the much-needed help for these children.

I have met bright children who are being assessed as 'slow learners' or misdiagnosed with ADHD because they are unable to express themselves correctly.

My character Omid is a lucky one. He receives an exceptional range of support and attention. I guess I hope his story might set a good example.

Most importantly I hope people, especially young people recognise, that even if they cannot communicate with us yet, these kids are just as ordinary as the rest of their friends. They too have a past, a life, grandparents that adored them and Aunties and Uncles who spoiled them. In short given a chance, they will be good friends and fun companions.

The story of the Rolling Pumpkin is an old folklore fairy-tale that my grandmother used to tell me when I was a child. My young hero, Omid clings to this fairy-tale throughout his story as his only connection to his past and beloved grandmother.

I am very grateful to all my friends, family and fellow students who read my story and provided me with feedback and encouragement. My son Keanu with his love for dinosaurs and mythical creatures has been a great inspiration. He even helped me pick the mythical creatures at the beginning of each chapter and provided some interesting paintings (a couple of them appear on the first page).

My special thanks must go to my friend Sharon for allowing me to use her beautiful painting as my cover, and editor and friend, Kelly Hatley, who did not give up on me. Without her support and persistence, this story would still be sitting in a forgotten folder on my computer.

If you are affected or want to find further support and information on these issues you can visit:

https://www.refugeecouncil.org.uk/

https://www.childrenssociety.org.uk/

https://www.savethechildren.org/

https://www.unhcr.org/

Ingram Content Group UK Ltd.
Milton Keynes UK
UKHW041523070723
424730UK00001B/31